Enough is Enough!

To celebrate 'the table', friendships, slow food with the rich sauce of conversation;
and for Fay (mum) and her two kilo (!) purchase of pâté at the market in Uzès.

SW

Scholastic Press
345 Pacific Highway
Lindfield NSW 2070
an imprint of Scholastic Australia Pty Limited (ABN 11 000 614 577)
PO Box 579
Gosford NSW 2250
www.scholastic.com.au

Part of the Scholastic Group
Sydney ● Auckland ● New York ● Toronto ● London
● Mexico City ● New Delhi ● Hong Kong ● Buenos Aires ● Puerto Rico

First published in 2003.
Text copyright © Scott Willis, 2003.
Cover and interior illustrations copyright © Jenna Packer, 2003.

National Library of Australia Cataloguing-in-Publication entry
    Willis, Scott, 1969- .
    Enough is enough.
    For pre-school children.
    ISBN 1 86504 576 4.
    ISBN 1 86504 577 2 (pbk.).
    1. Grocery shopping - Juvenile fiction. I. Packer, Jenna, 1967- .
    II. Title.
NZ823.2

Typeset in Palatino.

Printed in Singapore by Imago Productions.

10 9 8 7 6 5 4 3 2 1   3 4 5 6 7 / 0

Enough is Enough!

Scott Willis   ✦   Jenna Packer

A Scholastic Press book from Scholastic Australia

It was Henry and Zoë's first day in their new home,
in a new city, in a new country.

Zoë had to begin her new job straight away.

'Bye-bye, my darlings!' she called,
as she sped down the stairs.

Henry and Balthus looked at each other.

Who did they know?

What was there to see?

How would they make friends?

They could hear people talking down in the street,
and the strange language wafted up to the window.
Balthus cocked his ear.

'Wonderful,' murmured Henry.

First there was the shopping to do.

They followed the crowds, the smells and the colours
until they reached the market.
It filled the street, ran over the footpath
and backed up the alleys.

Balthus's nose twitched with excitement.

Everyone was talking, smiling and laughing.
But the more Henry tried to catch a word,
the less he understood.

Balthus plunged happily ahead and Henry followed.

Sardines, herrings, cod and flounder.

Oysters, mussels, cockles and abalone.

Squid, octopus, lobster and crayfish.

Every kind of fish (except *jellyfish*, of course!)

lay in front of the fishmonger.

'A piece of cod, two small herrings,

half-a-dozen oysters and some squid rings please,'

asked Henry politely.

The fishmonger looked puzzled.

Then, *slap* went a slice of tuna,

plop went a small octopus,

slither went six slippery trout and

squelch went seven large herrings on top.

'But …' stammered Henry. 'Oh well, thank you.

That will be more than enough.'

At the vegetable stall,
Henry smiled and nodded,
though he didn't understand
a word the vegetable seller said.

'Well, I see, thank you,' he said,
as she placed twenty artichokes,
some tomatoes, garlic, onions,
and eggplants in a bag.

'I must learn this language, Balthus;
I only wanted *two* artichokes really.'

'Do you have noodles?'
Henry asked the pasta seller,
waggling his finger
at the different types.

Her eyes twinkled
as he pointed.
'Ah, spaghetti! Gnocchi!
Fettuccine! Ravioli! Rigatoni!
Macaroni! Tortellini!' she cried,
and her tongs snapped *click clack*
as she served him some of each.

'Can't have too much pasta, I suppose,' laughed Henry.
'But how to say "enough" if I need to?'

'Now, bread, Balthus—do we need bread?'

They looked at the fat floury loaves,
the long skinny loaves, the ficelles,
and the focaccias with dents and olives and nuts and knots.
Each time they pointed, the big floury baker picked up a loaf,
until Henry found he had chosen fifteen different kinds of bread.

'What will we put on so much bread, Balthus?'

But Balthus was already following his nose.

Henry followed until—'Oh . . .

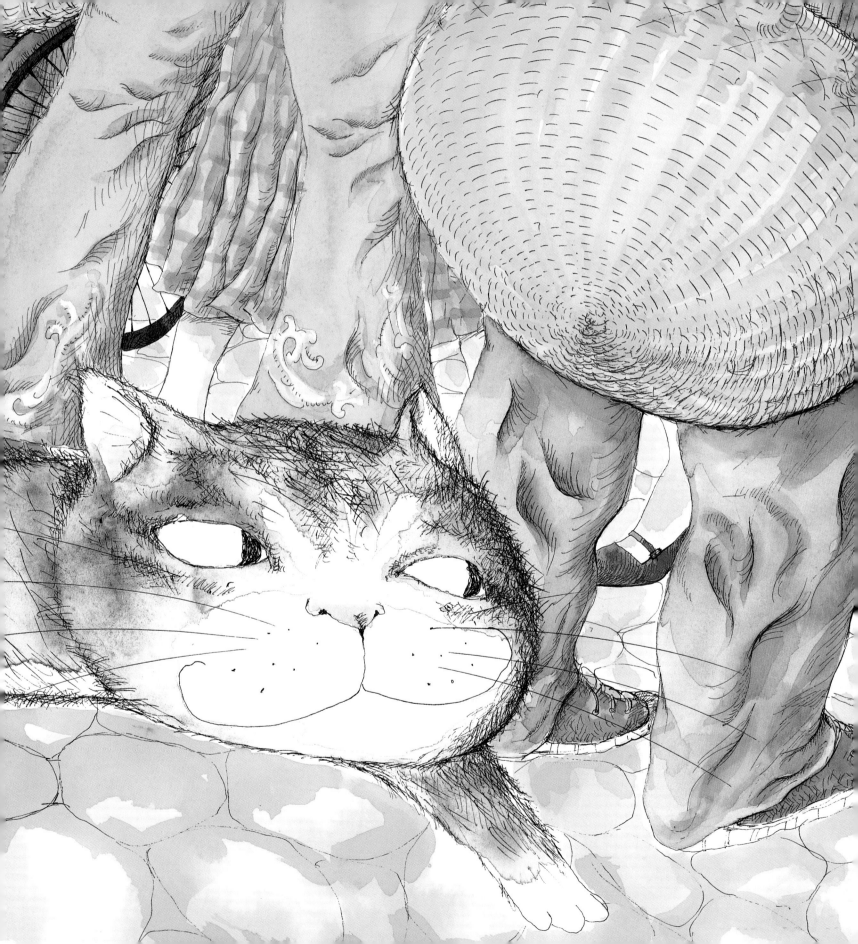

'Cheeses!' Cheeses here, cheeses there,
chunks of cheese everywhere!
Goat's cheese, sheep's cheese, cow's cheese—
Henry's nose filled with stinky, wonderful smells.

Before he knew it, he had chosen a pile of pélardons,
a gob of gorgonzola, half a wheel of yellow gouda,
some creamy camembert and a very smelly munster.

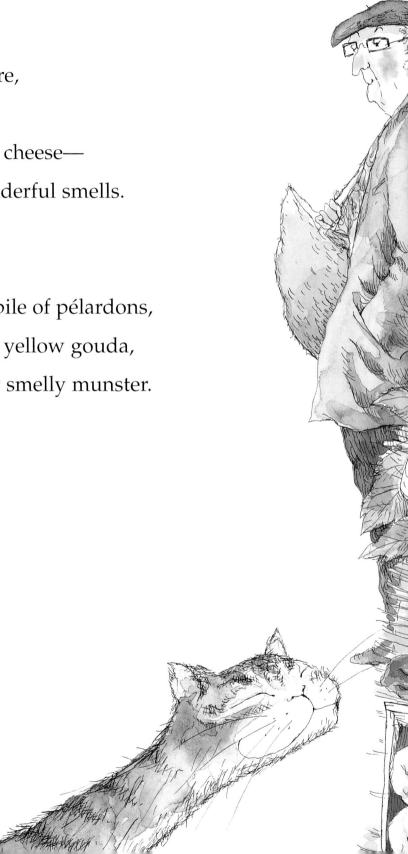

The olive seller next-door offered
Henry some olives to taste.

There were *mmm!* large green olives and
yum! small black ones and
oh! fat purple ones and
ouch! chilli hot ones—for Zoë.
The pile got bigger as Henry pointed to
each tub in turn.

'It seems we're getting
the hang of it, Balthus,' he laughed.
'Come on, lend a paw, it's getting late!'

Henry piled the baskets of shopping onto the vespa.

Where was that cat?

'Trust Balthus to disappear just when I need some help.

He must have gone already!' Henry sped home over the cobbles.

After the bustle of the market,

the building seemed cool and quiet and lonely.

'Balthus!' Henry called,

but there was no reply.

What a lot of bundles!
Henry tottered up the first step,
teetered at the next and then,
just as he caught his balance,
he stumbled, tripped
and dropped everything.

'Oh dear, oh dear!' he exclaimed.
Doors opened one by one,
and curious faces peered out.

Henry's new neighbours helped him to his feet,
then helped pick up the shopping, piece by piece,
and carried it up the stairs.

Zoë was already home.
'Hello, darling,' she said,
then stared in astonishment.
'But Henry—enough is enough!
How are we going to eat all that?'

'Don't worry,' said Henry,
'we'll need it all.
I've made some new friends—
and they're coming to dinner!'

They'd never had such a feast.

Henry squeezed Zoë's hand.

'What a wonderful first day,' he sighed.

'But I wonder what's become of Balthus?

He's bound to be hungry!'